Rain, Ra

Written by Jill Eggleton
Illustrated by Philip Webb

"I am wet,"
said the giraffe.

"I am wet,"
said the lion.

"I am wet,"
said the tiger.

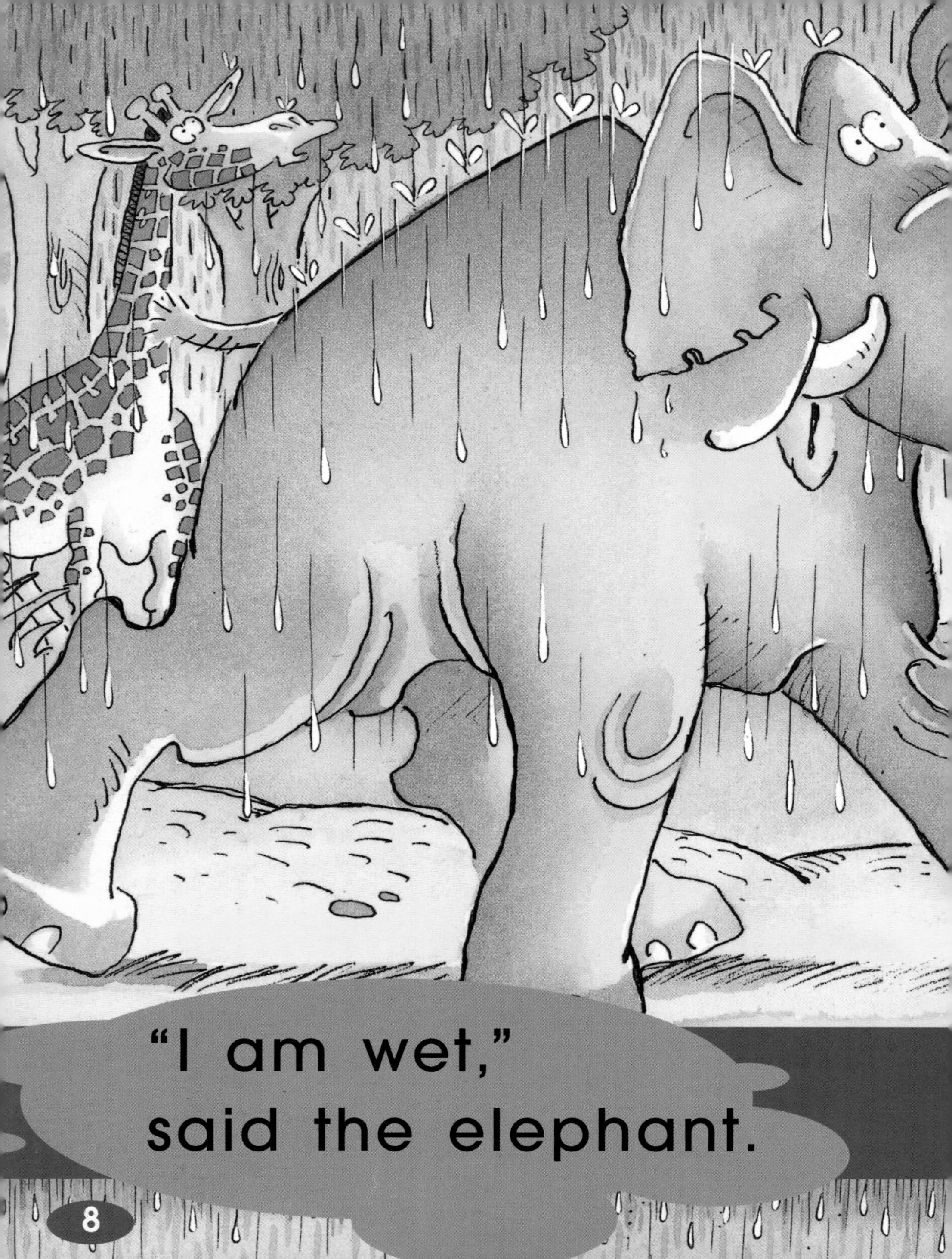

"I am wet,"
said the elephant.

“I am **not** wet,”
said the mouse.

Oops!

"I am squashed!"

A Story Sequence

1

2

3

4
5
6

Guide Notes

Title: Rain, Rain, Rain
Stage: Emergent – Magenta

Genre: Fiction
Approach: Guided Reading
Processes: Thinking Critically, Exploring Language, Processing Information
Written and Visual Focus: Story Sequence
Word Count: 35

Forming the Foundation

Tell the children that the story is about animals who are standing in the rain getting wet. The mouse in the story finds a way to keep dry.
Talk to them about what is on the front cover. Read the title and the author/illustrator.
"Walk" through the book, focusing on the illustrations and talking to the children about what is happening in each spread.
Leave pages 12-13 for prediction.

Read the text together.

Thinking Critically

(sample questions)

After the reading

- Where do you think the animals could have gone to get dry?
- What do you think the animals could be thinking about the mouse?

Exploring Language

(ideas for selection)

Terminology
Title, cover, author, illustrator, illustrations

Vocabulary
Interest words: wet, giraffe, lion, tiger, elephant, mouse, squashed, not
High-frequency words: I, am, said, the